Rattle and Hum
in Double Trouble

Frank Rodgers

Collins

Look out for more *Jets* from Collins

First published by A & C Black Ltd in 1997
Published by Collins in 1998
10 9 8 7 6 5 4 3 2
Collins is an imprint of HarperCollins*Publishers* Ltd,
77–85 Fulham Palace Road, Hammersmith, London W6 8JB

ISBN 0 00 675324 8

© 1997 Frank Rodgers

Frank Rodgers asserts the moral right to be identified as
the author and the illustrator of the work.
A CIP record for this title is available from the British Library.
Printed and bound in Great Britain by Clays Ltd, St Ives plc

Chapter One

Rattle and Hum,
robot detectives,
were rattling
and humming
twice as loud
as usual.

'What's the matter with you both?'
demanded Sergeant Salt, who was
trying to have a quiet cup of tea and
a biscuit.

Got ants in your pants?

CLANG! CLANG!

'Whoops!' said Rattle and Hum as
their bottoms fell off.

'Perhaps I shouldn't have mentioned
pants,' sighed the sergeant.

'We're sorry, Sergeant,' said Rattle and Hum, picking up their bottoms and fixing them back on.

'But there's a strange feeling in the air this morning.'

Sergeant Salt was not amused.

Rattle and Hum hurried out of the door, clutching on to their bottoms.

But as they walked through the town they found that strange things were happening everywhere.

The hairdryers in Maison Toupé had gone haywire.

The cars in Stan and Oily's showroom had driven off by themselves.

And, with no one near it, Cannonball Kate's cutlass had shot across the Treasure Island Cafe, giving two customers a centre parting.

Kate was not amused either.
'As if I didn't have enough problems!' she yelled.

Rattle and Hum set off, completely forgetting that they were supposed to be on their way to the Robot Factory for urgent repairs.

But when they arrived at Bubbly's, they found that she was having a difficult morning as well.

'There's something very strange going on,' she cried as the robots came up the path.

My pets shot up the chimney a moment ago and landed in the garden!

'So you haven't been trying out some new spells then?' said Rattle.

'Certainly not!' replied Bubbly.

'Fascinating,' said Bubbly. 'Pity I can't stop to talk about it, but I've got a date with Ernest at Kate's cafe.'

'Mr Gumboyle?! Uh-oh! That reminds me,' said Hum. 'We're supposed to be at the Robot Factory. Let's go!'

Chapter Two

Ahh...bliss!

Back at the Police Station, Sergeant Salt had just made himself another cup of tea. He opened his copy of the police newspaper and began to read.

The Jaily News — — — — — — — — — Issue No. 1345 — — —

POWER-MAD INVENTOR HEADING THIS WAY.

Dr Jermy Vyrus says he wants to take over the world!

Last week, the power-mad inventor built a robot prime minister so that it could run the country for him.

Nobody could tell the difference between the real one and the robot until, luckily, the robot's head fell off.

All police are warned to keep watch at their local Robot Factory as Dr Vyrus may cause trouble there!

splutter

Keep watch at the Robot Factory?

Ah... it's all right. I've just remembered. I sent Rattle and Hum there...

...to be repaired! They're falling apart! They'll be useless!

He grabbed his jacket and rushed out.

Police Station

I must warn Mr Gumboyle!

Chapter Three

Meanwhile, at the Robot Factory, Rattle and Hum had been met by Mr Gumboyle and Ernest. Mr Gumboyle had once been bad-tempered and nasty, but one of Bubbly's spells had turned him into a nice person.

'I'll just go and get some tools,' said
Mr Gumboyle, and he left the room.
But almost immediately, he came
back in through another door, and he
seemed to be in a terrible rage.

'B..b..but,' stammered Ernest, very
confused, 'didn't you just..?'

'Are you interrupting me, Pimm?'
snarled Mr Gumboyle.

Mr Gumboyle stormed out, leaving Rattle and Hum and Ernest looking at each other in amazement.

Wh...what's got into Mr Gumboyle?

Perhaps Bubbly spell has worn off?

Then the door opened again, and Mr Gumboyle came in, all smiles.

Won't keep you long! I'm just looking for a special tool.

Ernest...why don't you make Rattle and Hum a nice pot of hot engine oil while they're waiting? I won't be a tick.

He gave Rattle and Hum a big smile and left the room.

Ernest and Rattle and Hum were dumbstruck.

But before they could utter a word, Mr Gumboyle rushed in once more.

Then the door opened <u>again</u> and in came...

...*another* Mr Gumboyle!

Rattle and Hum stared in astonishment, and Ernest nearly fainted.

Who are you?!

Who are you?!

I asked first!

All right, then... I'm Mr Gumboyle, Director of this Robot Factory!

But you can't be! I'm Mr Gumboyle!

No you're not!

Yes I am!

No you're not!

'This could go on forever!' wailed Ernest. 'What shall we do?'

It's a mystery, Rattle...

And we're good at solving mysteries, Hum!

But before they could give it another thought, the door opened again...

19

...and Sergeant Salt rushed in.
'I've come to warn you, Mr Gumboyle!'
he cried...then skidded to a halt in
mid-sentence.

'B..but I can't tell you apart,' stammered the sergeant.

'Oh dear,' thought Sergeant Salt. 'Bubbly's spell must have worn off. This nasty one must be the real Mr Gumboyle.' Quickly he put handcuffs on the other Mr Gumboyle.

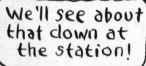

'You are going to jail, my lad,' said the sergeant grimly. 'I'll soon find out what's going on.'

He turned to the other Mr Gumboyle as he went out.

The remaining Mr Gumboyle grinned at Rattle and Hum as Sergeant Salt left.

'Oh yes,' he smirked. 'I'll make sure they're fixed...'

PERMANENTLY!

He glared at Ernest. 'And as for you,' he snapped, 'get back to work!'

Diagram of inside Ernest's brain.

It's a TWISTER!

Ernest's brain was in a whirl. All he could think of to say was, 'Er...yes, Mr Gumboyle, but remember we have a lunch date at the Treasure Island Cafe.'

Once in the repair room, Mr Gumboyle clamped Rattle and Hum into the automatic repair machine.

'This won't hurt a bit,' he smirked, and he set the dial to...

As he went out he waved to Rattle and Hum. 'So sorry to leave,' he sniggered. 'I'm all broken up about it. But then again, SO WILL YOU BE! Ha Ha!'

Chapter Four

At 12 o'clock, Mr Gumboyle and Ernest arrived at the Treasure Island Cafe. Kate was rushing about serving lunch.

She fluttered her eyelashes at Mr Gumboyle.

'Not hungry,' snarled Mr Gumboyle.
'Not hungry...not hungry...not...'

'What?' asked Kate, amazed.

'Not hungry...not hungry...' repeated
Mr Gumboyle like a broken record
until Ernest gave him a little shake.

When her guests had gone a tear
trickled down Kate's face.

Gumsy-Wumsy just didn't seem his old self today.

He's never refused my pancakes and syrup before. *NEVER!*

They're his favourites! Maybe that means he doesn't love me any more. *BOO HOO!*

But then she remembered what
Ernest had said before he left.

We had double trouble at the Factory today, Kate. There were TWO Mr Gumboyles! Sgt Salt arrested the other one!

Kate stopped crying.

Of course! How silly of me! This Mr Gumboyle must be the fake. My real Gumsy-Wumsy is in jail!

Chapter Five

Down at the Police Station, Sergeant Salt had just made himself another cup of tea when **CRASH!** the door flew open.

Avast there, you jail-lubber! You've a-got the wrong man! The Mr Gumboyle in the cells is innocent!!

'Really?' spluttered the sergeant. 'How do you know?'

'I just know!' roared Kate. 'Take my word for it!'

'I'm sorry, madam,' said Sergeant Salt stiffly, 'but I'll need proof before I can release him. Do you have proof?'

Of course I haven't! I just know! It's female pirate intuition!

Er...that's not good enough, I'm afraid.

Sergeant Salt landed on his bottom
with a thump and immediately Kate
was sorry.

The sergeant got to his feet and led
Kate off to the cells.

Chapter Six

Back at the Robot Factory, things weren't going well either. Ernest couldn't find Rattle and Hum anywhere, and to make matters worse, Mr Gumboyle turned really nasty.

'Don't argue with me, Pimm...just do it!' roared the director.

Ernest began to load the plans into the computer.

Suddenly Ernest gasped.

Ernest glanced over his shoulder.
The imposter wasn't looking...

...so he quickly made a few changes to the plans as he put them into the computer.

Right, keep at it! I'll be back later to see how you're getting on.

As soon as Mr Gumboyle left the room, Ernest scuttled to the back door. 'Now's my chance to warn Sergeant Salt,' he thought. But as he passed the rubbish bins he heard a strange noise.

CLUNK!

Where did that come from?

In here

Ernest lifted the lids.

'I've got to get you out of here before the fake Mr Gumboyle arrives!' he cried. Ernest backed up his car, and loaded the bins into the boot. Then he jumped in and drove off...fast!

Chapter Seven

Ernest screeched to a halt outside
Bubbly's house. Quickly he explained
what had happened, then he and
Bubbly lifted the bins into the garden.

You're the only one who can put Rattle and Hum together again quickly, Bubbly. It would take me weeks!

Oh dear I'm afrai my mag is a bi rusty

'But I'll give it a try,' she said.

I wish I could cross my fingers!

Bubbly waved her hands in the air.

'Looks like it should be in an art gallery,' said Ernest.

'Whoops! I'll try again,' said Bubbly.

'Er...one more try?' said Bubbly.

'Now,' said Rattle, 'let's try and solve this mystery of the two Mr Gumboyles.'

Perhaps it's connected in some way with all the electrical activity.

Hum tapped a few keys on Rattle's chest keyboard and...

ZZZZZZZ₀₀₀

...out came a map of the town. On it were marked the places affected by the surge of electricity.

'Perhaps that's the source of the problem,' suggested Rattle.

'We'll soon find out,' replied Hum and turned to Bubbly. 'Why don't you go and tell Sergeant Salt what has happened and we'll go and investigate this building with Ernest.'

'Right you are,' replied Bubbly, and everyone set off.

Chapter Eight

Bubbly burst into the Police Station like a tornado. 'Sergeant Salt! The Mr Gumboyle at the factory is a fake!'

'Wasn't Kate's word good enough?' cried Bubbly in amazement.

'Without proof...I'm afraid not,' the sergeant gulped in embarrassment.

'Ooooh!' cried Bubbly in frustration. 'If you don't release him I'll do it myself!'

Sergeant Salt didn't know what
to do.

Chapter Nine

Meanwhile, Rattle and Hum and
Ernest had arrived at the building
they suspected of being the source of
the electrical activity.

Look... there are flashes of light coming from that open door in the basement!

Quietly, all three crept down the
stairs and peered round the door.

In the middle of the room stood a huge machine, spitting sparks. Beside it stood a man pushing buttons.

Just then another door opened and in came the fake Mr Gumboyle with some nasty-looking robots.

'Splendid!' replied Jermy Vyrus. 'But I see your voice module isn't working properly. Step inside the Replicator, and I'll have you fixed in no time.'

Mr Gumboyle stepped inside the machine...

...and stepped out a moment later.

Outside the door, Rattle and Hum and Ernest watched in amazement.

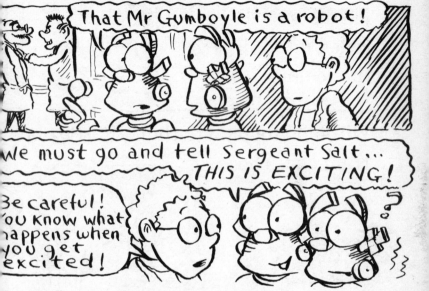

The robots began to rattle and hum loudly.

They clutched at their bottoms but it was too late...

CLANG! CLANG!

...their bottoms fell off and rolled into the room.

BOINK!

Without stopping to think, Rattle and Hum gave chase.

INTRUDERS!

It's those two metal nosy-parker Rattle and Hum, the robot detectives

Rattle and Hum caught their bottoms...but then <u>they</u> were caught by the nasty robots...

...who locked them in a cage in the corner of the room with Ernest.

Chapter Ten

Back at the Police Station, things were just as gloomy.

Shiver me Kitchens
This is a fine
pickle we're in!

'Oh, I know,' moaned Bubbly, 'and I'm so worried about poor Ernest, and Rattle and Hum. I wish I knew what was happening to them.'

Don't you have a crystal ball, Bubbly? I thought all witches had them?

Of course! It's in my pocket!

Good for you Gumsy!

She pulled it out and gazed into its glassy depths.

Crystal, crystal, shaped like a ball... Can you tell me what's happened to Ernest, at all?

Bubbly and Kate gasped at what they saw.

What is it?!

Rattle and Hum and Ernest are behind bars just like us! They've been caught by the fake Mr Gumboyle!

'What is it?' grumbled the sergeant, wiping tea and biscuit from the front of his uniform for the sixth time that day.

Sergeant Salt's jaw dropped.

It's Jermy Vyrus, the power-mad inventor!

Oh dear... I've been a silly sergeant. He's been behind it all along!

I have got the wrong man in jail!

'Of course you have!' snapped Kate, taking Mr Gumboyle's hand. 'How could you have ever thought that my Gumsy-Wumsy was a fake?'

'I...I'm sorry,' stammered the sergeant, letting them out of jail.

Now...come on everyone... we've got to save Ernest and Rattle and Hum! LET'S GO!

Chapter Eleven

Meanwhile, at Jermy Vyrus's laboratory, Hum had been studying the lock on the cage.

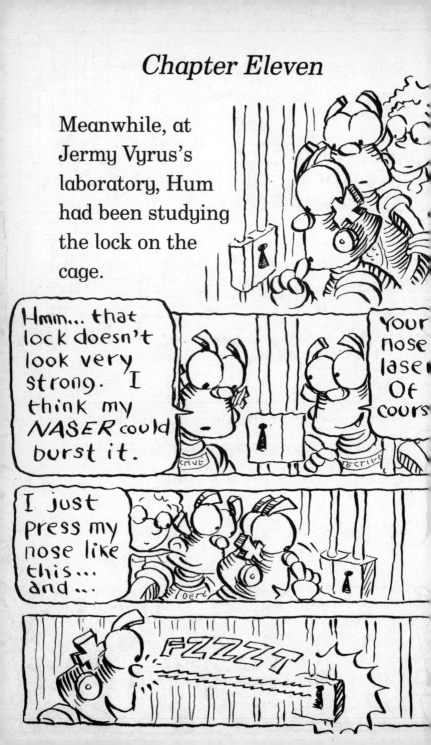

Hmm... that lock doesn't look very strong. I think my *NASER* could burst it.

Your nose lase Of cours

I just press my nose like this... and...

FZZZT

There was a click and the door swung open. At the same moment, there was a loud **CRASH!** and in charged Kate, Bubbly, Sergeant Salt and Mr Gumboyle.

Avast! Ye rabble o' rotten robots! Kate's a-going to knock your blocks off!!

Kate charged at the nasty robots but suddenly skidded to a halt as something rather strange started to happen.

The nasty robots began to fall apart.

Rattle and Hum clutched at their bottoms just in case.

Ernest laughed.

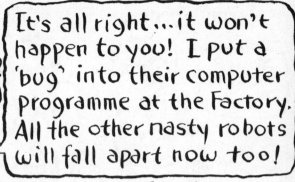

It's all right...it won't happen to you! I put a 'bug' into their computer programme at the Factory. All the other nasty robots will fall apart now too!

HOORAY! Ernest is our hero!!

He's always been my hero!

A sudden noise made Hum whirl round.

QUICK!! ...he robot Mr ...umboyle and ...ermy Vyrus ...re escaping!

Sergeant Salt prepared to take Jermy Vyrus off to jail. 'What should we do with the robot Mr Gumboyle?' he whispered to Rattle and Hum.

He could be re-programmed...

...and turned into a nice person.

'I've got an idea!' cried Kate. 'He could be a waiter in my cafe!'

He would always remind me of the real thing!

The real Mr Gumboyle blushed.

Kate suddenly snapped her fingers.

Shiver me brainwaves! I've got another idea! Not only do I need a waiter... I also need a chef...

She pointed at Jermy Vyrus. 'Why not have him do community service in my kitchen instead of going to jail? It would be a perfect job for someone who is power-mad!'

Jermy Vyrus couldn't believe his luck.

A CHEF!? Oh yes, that would be super-brill! I've always wanted to be in charge of a kitchen!

Oh, Ms Cannonball...

I'll invent so many amazing new dishes for you... the Treasure Island Café will be the most famous café in town!

Sergeant Salt was delighted with both ideas and agreed at once.

Jermy Vyrus quickly re-programmed his fake Mr Gumboyle in the Replicator machine...

...then they all went to the Treasure Island Cafe where Jermy Vyrus and his robot became chef and waiter.

After having a tasty tea of cakes, pancakes, syrup and hot engine oil, Rattle and Hum went back to the police station with Sergeant Salt.

'And it looks like you two don't need repairing after all!' said the sergeant.

He clapped Rattle and Hum on the back so hard that...

...their bottoms fell off again.

'Time for a cup of tea and a biscuit,'
sighed the sergeant.